STORIES FOR CHILDREN EVERYWHERE

CLIVEDEN PRESS

CONTENTS

RUMPELSTILTSKIN

There was once a poor miller who had a beautiful daughter. He was so proud of Gisella that he would sing his daughter's praises to anyone who had the time to listen.

"She is as clever as she is beautiful," he would boast. "Why, even though she is the daughter of a poor miller she is a fit bride for the king himself!"

"You should tell the king that," laughed a bluff old farmer who came to the mill to have his corn ground into flour. "He comes to hunt here often."

"I might just do that," retorted the miller, who was a rather vain and proud man who hated anyone to laugh at him. "You may mock now, but just wait and see."

Several days passed by and then one morning, as he was working in his mill, the miller heard the sound of hunting horns. He remembered what the old farmer had said, and he rushed outside eagerly.

And there in a clearing near the mill sat the young king, astride a fine horse.

"Good day, sire," cried the miller, bowing low.

"Good day to you, Miller," replied the king.

He was about to ride on when the miller added quickly, "I have a beautiful daughter, sire, who is very clever."

"Indeed?" said the king politely. "There are many beautiful and clever girls in my kingdom."

The miller hesitated and then he added quickly, "My daughter can spin straw into gold!"

"Straw into gold?" echoed the king. "That is indeed a wonder, Master Miller. It is so difficult to believe that I should like to see this for myself . . . and add more gold to my coffers. Tell your daughter to come to my castle tomorrow and I shall put her to the test. But take care that you do not jest, Master Miller. I don't like to be mocked or deceived by my subjects. If your daughter cannot spin straw into gold both of you will be sorry for your vain boast!"

As the king rode off, the miller gazed after him with some misgivings. What had he done? Then, thinking how clever his daughter was, the miller was confident that somehow she would achieve the impossible and manage to convince the king that she could spin straw into gold.

Gisella was horrified when she discovered
what her father had said to the king, but she was
a dutiful daughter, and the next morning she
presented herself at the castle gates and asked
to see the king.

"You are indeed as beautiful as your father
said," said the king, as he led the miller's
daughter along long, winding passages in a
turreted tower. "Now, let me see if he spoke
the whole truth. Spin this straw into gold for me."

Gisella gazed in dismay at the great quantity
of straw piled up high all over the room, and the
spinning wheel which stood close by.

"If you value your freedom do not fail," said
the king sternly. "I do not like idle boasts, and
we have dark dungeons for those who make
them. I will return at sunrise tomorrow, and I
will expect this room to be filled with gold."

And with these words the king left Gisella
alone, locking the door as he went out.

Poor Gisella sat down at the spinning wheel and tried to spin. But the straw fell off the spindle and cut her finger with its roughness.

"Oh, Father, what have you done?" she sobbed. "I cannot make straw into gold, and tomorrow our lives may be forfeit for your vain boast. We cannot expect any mercy from the king. He will be so angry when he finds out how we have deceived him. Oh, if only I had someone to turn to for help. But I am locked in, alone and friendless!"

But, as she finished speaking, to her great amazement Gisella saw the locked door open, and in walked a tiny dwarf.

"Good day, my child," said the dwarf. "I heard you ask for help. Why are you crying?"

"Because the king has given me the impossible task of spinning straw into gold," cried the miller's daughter. "And since I cannot do this, tomorrow my life will end!"

"Nay, not so," replied the dwarf, seating himself at the spinning wheel. "I can spin straw into gold, but what will you give me in return for my labours?"

"You shall have my pretty scarf!" cried Gisella. "But please hurry, for the king will return at sunrise!"

The dwarf took the scarf eagerly, and he spun the wheel swiftly three times until the spindle was full. Then, as he worked, Gisella saw the straw turn to glittering gold. Round and round went the wheel and, as dawn broke, the last spindle was filled with sparkling gold.

"There, it is done! Now I must go, for I hear the king approaching," cried the dwarf, rising to his feet.

Gisella stammered her thanks as she looked towards the door. But when she looked again at the golden spindles, the dwarf had vanished. He was nowhere to be seen at all!

With a tiny smile Gisella said demurely: "Enter, sire, here is your gold."

The king could scarcely believe his eyes when he saw all the gold and not even one wisp of straw remaining.

"It is magic!" he cried in delight, fingering the gold. "Your father spoke naught but the truth. You are indeed a clever maiden. I will send my servants to put this gold in my treasure house to keep it safe from thieves."

"I am glad you are pleased, sire," said Gisella. "But now may I return home to my father?"

The miller's daughter expected the king to agree, but he shook his head, for although he was wealthy, the king loved gold.

"Not yet," said the king. "First you must eat and sleep. You must be tired after your night's work."

Gisella was indeed tired, for although she had not spun the gold herself, she had sat up all night watching the dwarf at work. So she gratefully accepted the king's offer to get some rest.

She was taken to a pretty bedchamber where she slept in a very comfortable bed with silken covers, and when she awoke, a servant brought the miller's daughter a delicious meal of food such as she had never even tasted before.

Gisella was just beginning to think that all had worked out well when she was summoned to see the king again . . . and what a shock awaited the poor girl!

The king took Gisella into yet another room filled with straw and ordered her to spin it into gold.

Once more Gisella began to weep, but again the dwarf appeared and offered to spin the straw into gold in return for the pretty ring which she wore on her finger.

Gisella gave the dwarf the ring immediately, and he set to work at once.

When the king returned at sunrise, there was the gold once more.

But the sight of the gold made the king demand even more, and the next night he ordered Gisella to spin more straw into gold, promising that if she did it a third time, he would ask no more and he would make her his queen.

But this time Gisella had nothing to give the dwarf for his labours and he refused to spin the straw.

Gisella began to cry, and at last the dwarf's heart softened.

"Very well," he said. "I will spin the straw for the last time, but in return you must promise me your first-born child when you become queen."

Gisella realised that she must give her word if the task was to be completed. So she nodded, thinking that she was not even the king's wife yet.

So the dwarf sat down at the spinning wheel and spun even more gold than ever before, much to the delight of the king when he arrived almost before the sun was up next morning.

"You have proved that you are a fit bride for me," cried the king. "Now we have the richest kingdom of all, with enough gold to last during not only our lives, but those of our children and our grand-children!"

Gisella felt a touch of fear at these words, remembering her promise to the dwarf. But she forgot all about the dwarf as preparations began for the wedding.

It was a wonderful wedding and none of the guests was more proud than the miller, who could now boast proudly and truthfully that his beautiful daughter was a queen among women.

But not even to her proud father did Gisella confide the secret of who really had spun all the straw into gold.

Instead, with her gracious ways and merry smiles she won the hearts of all at court, and her handsome young husband came to love her more dearly as each day passed.

The days passed happily for Gisella, and about a year after their marriage a child was born to the young couple and all the people in the land rejoiced at this happy news.

But one day, as the young queen sat nursing her baby in the royal garden, the little dwarf suddenly appeared before her.

"Good day, Your Majesty," he said with a little smile. "I see that the king, like myself, kept his promise and made you his queen. Now the time has come for you to keep the promise you made to me when I spun the straw into gold for you. I have come for your first-born child."

The young queen was filled with horror. She offered the dwarf any of the riches in the royal treasure chest instead. But he refused.

"A living child is dearer to me than cold hard jewels," he replied.

But as the queen began to weep, he said, "But I am a fair fairy man. I will give you three days in which to find out my name. If you can do this, you may keep your child, and I will trouble you no more. I will come each day to hear your guess, and on the third day, the child will be mine."

As the dwarf vanished from sight, the queen held her baby tightly, and she resolved at all cost to find out the name of the dwarf.

She sent messengers to all parts of the kingdom, asking them to seek out unusual names. She pretended that she wished to know the names in case there was one she might like to give her baby.

The messengers were rather puzzled by the queen's request, but they wanted to please her, so they set about the strange task willingly.

They brought back many names and on the first night, the queen said to the dwarf: "Is your name Gooseneck . . . or Spindleshanks . . . is it Peppercorn . . . or Spiderlegs?"

"Nay, lady, none of those!" laughed the dwarf. "Try harder tomorrow!"

The next day the queen went all over her own city asking people their names.

Tailors and tinkers, soldiers and farriers, kitchenmaids and cooks, all came up to talk to their dear queen, who eagerly asked them their names and the names of their children.

"Well, Lady Queen, what say you tonight?" asked the dwarf on the second night.

"Are you called Gold Spinner?" asked the queen eagerly. "Or Treasure Man . . . or Money-bags?"

"That is not my name, but it was a brave try! But remember there's only one more night, lady," laughed the dwarf, and the poor queen started to sob bitterly as he vanished once more.

The queen hardly slept that night, and she looked so pale that the king feared she was ill and begged her to see the royal physician.

But the miller's daughter shook her head and went to sit alone in the garden.

It was here, in a little summerhouse, that the last messenger found her when he finally arrived back from the farthest part of the kingdom.

"I have only brought back one name, Your Majesty," he said, "but I have a very strange tale to tell. In the forest on the high hill I climbed a tree to rest a while, hoping to keep myself safe from wild animals. And there, in a clearing where the fox and the hare say goodnight, I saw a little house with a fire burning outside. A tiny man danced around this fire calling:

"Today I brew, tomorrow I bake,
For soon a royal child I'll take,
For neither man, king, queen or dame,
Know Rumpelstiltskin is my name!"

"May heaven reward you!" cried the radiant queen. "You have made me the happiest woman on earth."

"Well, My Lady Queen, what names have you before I take your child?" asked the dwarf when he appeared that night.

"Is your name Greybeard . . . Redcap . . . Kaspar . . . Hans . . ." began the queen.

"Enough, you will never guess," cried the dwarf, stretching out his hands towards the royal cradle.

"Is it Rumpelstiltskin?" cried the queen.

"The devil told you!" screamed the dwarf in rage, and he stamped his feet so hard that a great hole appeared and he disappeared beneath the ground and was never seen on earth again.

So the king and the miller's daughter lived happily together for many years, and the miller boasted to everyone how his daughter could turn straw into gold . . . but neither he nor the king ever discovered how Gisella had done it. It was a secret the miller's daughter never told anyone!

The Ant and the Grasshopper

One warm summer's day a Grasshopper was playing happily in a cornfield when he saw an Ant dragging a large grain of corn, larger than the insect itself, along a narrow path.

"It is too hot to work!" laughed the Grasshopper. "Why don't you rest in the shade?"

"Because I must prepare for winter," replied the Ant. "There will be no food to be got then, so I am building up a store now. I advise you to do the same, my friend!"

But the Grasshopper laughed again.

"Winter is a long way off!" he cried. "I will worry about it when it comes."

"You are a very foolish creature," replied the Ant, as he pushed his heavy burden further along the pathway.

At last winter came, and because he had a full food store the cold winds did not harm the Ant.

But the Grasshopper had no food, and when he asked the Ant for a grain of corn, the Ant replied sternly, "You played all summer, now you must go hungry all winter. Now you have learned that it is best to prepare ahead for any difficulties which you can forsee in the future!"

The Lion and the Mouse

One day as a magnificent Lion lay sleeping in a clearing in the middle of a forest a tiny Mouse ran over the Lion's paw. Angry at being awoken, the Lion seized the Mouse and he was just about to crush the tiny creature when the Mouse cried out, "Please spare me, mighty King of the Jungle, and perhaps one day I may save your life!"

The Lion roared with laughter at this suggestion, but he decided that since the Mouse was scarcely a mouthful to eat he might as well let him go.

Some time later, as the Lion was searching the forest for food he was suddenly trapped in a hunter's net. The more he struggled, the tighter the net grew, and he roared with rage at the thought of the fate which lay ahead of him.

But the Lion's roars were heard by the Mouse who ran to the Lion's aid. The Mouse's sharp teeth quickly gnawed through the ropes of the net and soon the Lion was freed.

"There you are!" cried the Mouse. "You laughed when I said I might help you some day! Now you will always remember that even the smallest of creatures can help the largest in certain circumstances."

And the grateful Lion was all too willing to agree!

To Mouse
with thanks —
Leo.

The Town Mouse and the Country Mouse

Once, deep in the heart of the country, there stood a poor farm. On the farm there stood a large old barn, and in that barn lived a country mouse called Thomas.

Thomas was a happy and contented mouse. He spent most of his time out in the fields, scurrying here and there in search of food. Some days he would go into the corn fields to gather odd grains of oats and barley in the stubble, then on other days he would venture into the kitchen garden to see what he could find there. If he was lucky he would find a few peas or beans or the occasional lettuce leaf. Whatever he found Thomas carried carefully back to his home in the far corner of the barn, where he added it to his small larder.

When the farm was quiet in the evenings Thomas would wait until the last lamp went out, then he would creep into the kitchen to see what he could find. Sometimes it was a few crumbs of freshly-baked bread, sometimes a few morsels of tasty cheese. Whatever it was, Thomas would carry it carefully back home and add it to his larder.

In the autumn Thomas was particularly busy. Every day he would go out into the woods to gather acorns and nuts that had fallen from the trees, or berries that the birds had missed. All in all, Thomas's life was a happy and contented one – he had enough to eat and drink, and a warm bed of sweet-smelling hay to curl up in every night . . . .

22

But one thing was missing – a friend. Thomas was the only mouse for miles around, and he sometimes felt a little lonely. His only relative was his cousin, Sylvester, who lived in the big city. Thomas had never met Sylvester, so one day when he was feeling a little lonely he decided to ask Sylvester to stay with him in the country for a few days. "The country air will do you good," he wrote to his city cousin. "Please come, I would so much like to meet you."

Within a few days Thomas had Sylvester's reply: "I'd be delighted to visit you, cousin. I'll be there on Saturday afternoon."

Tom gulped. Saturday – that was tomorrow! Sylvester lived in a huge mansion in the best part of the city – what would he think of the humble barn? Thomas began to think that his idea had been a mistake, after all. But it was too late now. "I'll just have to do my best to make Sylvester's stay a pleasant one," he said. "I hope he won't be too disappointed . . . ."

Without wasting another second Thomas picked up a broom and brushed the floor of his home. Then he took a duster and dusted everything in sight. Everything had to be just right for Sylvester.

When the cleaning was finished Thomas dashed out of the barn and scurried and hurried through the fields, picking up a grain of wheat here, some oats there, even a large cabbage leaf from the kitchen garden. Then, when the farmhouse was dark and quiet, he crept into the kitchen and managed to find a piece of bacon rind and a corner of old cheese.

When he got back to the barn he laid out all the food in the larder and smiled. It wasn't grand, but there would be plenty to eat. Thomas hoped that he would make up in quantity what was lacking in quality.

On Saturday morning Thomas cleaned and dusted his home again, and waited impatiently at the top of the lane that led to the farm. Finally a small figure came into view, carrying a small suitcase. He was dressed in fine clothes and carried a cane with a gold knob on the top. It just had to be Sylvester....

Thomas shook his cousin's hand heartily. "Come into the barn, dear cousin," he said. "You must be tired after the journey. Sit down and I'll make tea." Sylvester looked disdainfully around the barn then walked to the rough table, dusting the chair with a lace-trimmed handkerchief before he sat down. "So this is your home, Thomas," he said. "Mmmmmm."

"Yes," said Thomas nervously. "It isn't very grand, I know, but, well, it's home. Now, let's have tea!"

Sylvester ate a morsel here and a crumb there, but didn't look very happy.

"Aren't you very hungry?" asked Thomas.

Sylvester turned up his rather long nose. "Yes, I am," he said, "but I really can't eat this. Is this the kind of food you have here in the country? Why, at my home I feast on lobster, beef and the finest wines and cheeses whenever I like. And it is so quiet here! In the city there are wide streets filled with horses, carriages and fine humans in beautiful clothes. Life in the country really cannot compare with life in the city!"

"No, I suppose it can't," said Thomas crestfallen. "But I rather *like* the country myself..."

"Oh, well, I'll only have to stay for a few days," said Sylvester. "Now, where's my bed? I'm rather tired."

Thomas showed Sylvester the heap of fresh straw he had arranged in a quiet corner. "Is this my bed?" asked Sylvester. "Why, I sleep on a bed of feathers in the city. Oh well, I suppose it will have to do." And with that he lay down and fell fast asleep.

26

In the morning the two cousins had breakfast, then Thomas showed Sylvester around the farm. Sylvester was not impressed. "But what on earth do you do all day?" he asked. "It's so *dull.*"

"I suppose it is, compared with the city," said Thomas, "but I keep myself busy. I gather food all day, take a stroll through the woods, have a chat to the geese on the pond . . . ."

"Then you don't know what you're missing," Sylvester interrupted. "Look, you must come back to the city with me. I'll show you riches and splendour that you've never even dreamed of. What do you say?"

"Well, I . . ."

"Splendid!" said Sylvester. "If we set off right away we'll reach the city tonight. Come on!"

It was growing dark when the two cousins reached the city, and Thomas was amazed at the strange noises he heard – the *clip clop* of horses' hooves, the rumble of the carriage wheels over the cobbles, the hundreds of different cries and voices. It certainly was very different after living in the country.

They crept stealthily along the gutters until they came to the great house where Sylvester lived. A clock struck eight as they ran down the drive, and Thomas jumped in alarm.

"It's only the clock," said Sylvester. "When the door opens, follow me inside."

As the great door opened the two mice darted inside and hid behind a marble pillar in the hall. Thomas peeped out and saw that the house was indeed just as splendid as Sylvester had said it would be – thick carpets covered Thomas's feet, and long velvet curtains hung from the vast windows. Huge chandeliers glittered from the ceiling, and the house seemed to stretch as far as the eye could see.

"Well, what do you think?" asked Sylvester.

Thomas was so impressed that he couldn't speak.

Sylvester smiled. "I'll show you the rest of the house," he said. "The humans are at the opera, so we won't be disturbed."

He led Thomas right through the great house until they came to the dining room. "Would you care for some supper?" he asked. "Just follow me." Sylvester scrambled up a tall chair leg and leapt onto the table, and Thomas followed.

What a sight! The huge table was filled with chickens and hams, joints of beef and bowls of salad and fruit. Seating his guest in the middle of the table with a large napkin around his neck, Sylvester ran here and there, bringing titbits for Thomas – lobster, turkey, creamy cakes and grapes. Thomas was overwhelmed – he had never tasted such delicious food in all his life.

"Better than your country fare, eh?" said Sylvester, and Thomas was just about to nod his head vigorously when a loud noise at the door made him start. "Quick!" said Sylvester. "The humans are back from the opera, and they're coming in here. Follow me!"

With that he leapt from the table and scrambled behind a heavy velvet curtain, dragging Thomas behind him. They heard the hum of voices, then another noise, a panting, snuffling noise. "What's that?" whispered Thomas, shaking with fright.

"It's the owners' dogs," said Sylvester, "and they hate mice. Keep absolutely still and quiet and we'll be alright. Don't utter a sound."

Thomas was so frightened that he couldn't have uttered a sound even if he had wanted to, and he stood very still for what seemed like hours. At last the sound of voices ceased, and the lights were switched off, and the two mice started to breathe again.

"It's safe now, the dogs will be in their baskets in the servants' quarters," said Sylvester. "I'll show you my home now."

Thomas was so frightened that he could hardly move, but he followed Sylvester as best he could, along the corridors, and down the stairs to the kitchens. Through a small hole in the skirting board they scurried, into a large hole furnished with the very best scraps of wallpaper and carpet. Thomas soon found himself lying in a bed of feathers in a matchbox, just as Sylvester had promised, but he did not sleep very well – he dreamed of the dogs that had so nearly caught him, and of the sweet-smelling hay back in the barn.

In the morning Sylvester roused his country cousin. "Come on, let's see if we can find something for breakfast."

33

Thomas followed him into the kitchen, and was just about to nibble up a crumb of brown bread from the floor when something caught his eye and made him stiffen with fright. It was a huge, black cat – and it was hurtling towards him! He ran as fast as he could for the garden door, with Sylvester close behind him, and he didn't stop running until he came to a crack in the high garden wall. He wriggled through it, then stood, panting, on the other side.

"That was close," said Sylvester. "That cat has nearly caught my tail a few times now."

"It was too close for me," said Thomas. "Thank you very much for your hospitality, cousin, but I think I'll go back home now. I may have only a humble home, and plain food to eat, but I'd rather have them than all the riches of the city. My life may be quiet, but at least I'm safe."

And with that the country mouse bade a fond farewell to his city cousin and hurried home as fast as his legs could carry him. He just couldn't wait to get back to his cosy home in the barn, and his bed of sweet-smelling hay . . . .

The Shepherdess and the Chimney Sweep

Imagine if you can a large room. In this room stood a big, black cabinet; a little old, a little shabby perhaps, but it was still a fine and imposing piece of furniture. The cabinet had stood in the room for many years, ever since the old lady who lived there was a young girl, with rosy cheeks and black hair.

The cabinet was beautifully carved, with designs of animals and flowers on each door. In the panel between the door was another carving of a full length figure of a man. At least, he was a sort of man, for he had the legs of a goat, short horns peeping through his curly hair and a long curly beard. He looked as if he was enjoying some kind of secret joke, for he was always smiling to himself.

The children who came to the house called him the Goatsleg High Adjutant Sergeant-Major, as they considered that a man with such an extraordinary appearance should have an extraordinary name.

Across the room from the cabinet was a table, and above the table was a looking glass. From where he stood, the Goatsleg High Adjutant Sergeant-Major could see his reflection. He could also see the prettiest little china shepherdess you have ever seen.

She made a charming picture, with her white skin faintly tinged with pink, her fair curls tied up with a blue ribbon and a deep red rose pinned to the lace on the front of her dress. In one tiny white hand she held a crook, while with the other she lifted the silken folds of her skirt in a graceful curtsey. Two dainty gilt slippers peeped out from the hem of her dress, and round her feet were clusters of delicate flowers.

When he wasn't looking at himself and admiring his fine figure, the Goatsleg High Adjutant Sergeant-Major would smile at the little shepherdess, but she had eyes for someone else.

Close by her on the table was another china figure: a chimney sweep. He was dressed in black from head to foot, with the exception of his white shirt, and the tools of his trade stood by him: his brushes, his ladder and his big sack. And yet, for all that he was a sweep, his skin was as pink and white as that of the shepherdess, and there wasn't a trace of soot to be seen anywhere.

The chimney sweep and the shepherdess were in love. They had stood together on the table since they first came to the house, and before that they had come from the same shop. They were even made from the same china. In other words they were well suited, and when the sweep asked the shepherdess to marry him she happily agreed.

On the same table, not far from the two little figures, sat an old Chinese mandarin. He too was made of china, but was very big and fat, and as he could nod his head he was thought to be very wise and was greatly respected.

The mandarin claimed that he was the grandfather of the little shepherdess, and although this was never proved he insisted that she was his responsibility. One day, the Goatsleg High Adjutant Sergeant-Major proposed to the little shepherdess, and the mandarin nodded his head in agreement.

The poor shepherdess tried to explain that she wished to marry the chimney sweep, but the mandarin said, "You should be very honoured by this offer.

The black cabinet is almost certainly made of mahogany and there is much silver inside, not to mention the valuables hidden in the secret drawer."

"That may be true," said the shepherdess, "but I have heard that he already has eleven china wives in that cabinet and, besides, I do not want to live in a dark cupboard."

But the mandarin would not listen. "As your grandfather it is for me to decide who marries you, and I say that you must accept the Goatsleg High Adjutant Sergeant-Major's offer. The wedding must be very . . . very . . . soon." The mandarin's head had begun to nod and soon he was asleep.

The shepherdess gave a little sob and ran back to the chimney sweep with tears streaming down her pink cheeks. "Take me away from here," she wept. "I will not marry that horrid man. Take me out into the wide world."

"Your wishes are mine also," said the sweep. "There are many chimneys to clean in the outside world, so I shall have plenty of work and we will not starve."

41

He took the shepherdess's hand and together they climbed down from the table. The shepherdess was rather frightened when she saw how far she had to go, but the sweep showed her where to put her feet and guided her safely to the floor.

Suddenly they heard the most terrible commotion, and when they looked round they saw that it was coming from the big black cabinet. The Goatsleg High Adjutant Sergeant-Major was almost beside himself with rage, leaping up and down and shouting at the old Chinese manadarin, who was still asleep. "They are running away! Stop them, they are running away!"

The young couple were frightened, and they looked desperately for somewhere to hide. "Quickly! Run to that cupboard under the windowseat," said the chimney sweep. "We'll hide there."

They scurried across to the windowseat and climbed into the cupboard. It was very crowded, as the dolls' theatre was putting on a play. The front seats were occupied by the kings and queens of hearts, diamonds, clubs and spades, while behind them sat the knaves who were acting as their pages. It was hot in the cupboard and they fanned themselves with flowers.

The play was about a young couple who loved each other and wished to be married, but their families kept them apart. The little china shepherdess felt very sad as it was her own story. "I can't bear to watch it," she wept. "Please let us leave here."

They pushed the cupboard door open and peeped round. To their horror they saw that the old mandarin had woken up and was shaking with rage.

"There is a big vase over there," said the sweep, pointing to a blue and white vase with a lid. "Perhaps we could hide in there."

But someone else had seen them escape. A big ginger cat sat in the shadows, and his green eyes narrowed with pleasure as he thought of the fun he would have with the little china figures. As the sweep and the shepherdess crept across the room he flexed his claws and prepared to pounce.

"Hurry, we are almost there," urged the sweep.

He looked anxiously over his shoulder and stared straight into the green eyes of the crouching cat. With a cry of alarm he grabbed the shepherdess's arm and pulled her away, just as the big cat sprang forward. The cat missed them, which made him furious, and as they ran trembling to the vase he crept up behind them.

Quickly the sweep lifted the lid off the blue and white vase. Then he almost carried the shepherdess, who was shaking with fear, and helped her inside. As he himself began to climb up, the cat pounced again, but the little sweep was too quick for him, and dropped down into the vase just as the cat's paw struck out.

The angry cat began to rock the vase, trying to tip the young couple out, and they clung to each other in terror. Surely they would never escape now. Fortunately, at that moment the owner of the house came into the room and saw what the cat was doing. "Stop that at once, you silly cat," she scolded. "Come with me and get your supper."

With a last nudge of his paw, the cat reluctantly followed his mistress out of the room and the sweep and the shepherdess breathed a sigh of relief.

45

They rested for a while, and then the shepherdess said, "I have been thinking about our problem, and I don't see how we can possibly stay here. No one will help us, as they all respect the old mandarin and dare not risk his anger, and soon that horrid cat will have finished his supper and will come back for us. No, there is nothing left for us but to go out into the wide world."

"Have you thought what that will mean?" said the little sweep. "The world is very large and very strange, and once we get there we won't be able to come back here ever again."

"I have thought of all that," said the shepherdess, "and I still feel that we must go."

The chimney sweep looked at her intently and then pointed to the chimney. "My way leads through there," he said. "I know the way well, and if you have the courage to follow me we will climb so high that they will never reach us, and at the top there is a hole that leads to the wide world."

They climbed cautiously down from the vase and crossed the room to the fireplace. "How dark it looks in there," said the shepherdess with a shiver, as she began to climb up the chimney behind the sweep.

"Stay close to me and you'll be quite safe," said the sweep. "It is not far now," he added to comfort her. "Look, there is a beautiful star shining above us."

It was a real star, and it shone down brightly on them, as if to show them the way.

The young couple climbed and climbed, up and up the black chimney, with the sweep helping the shepherdess at every step. At last they reached the top, and they climbed onto the edge of the chimney to rest, as they were very tired.

Above them was the great dome of the heavens, a dark cloak of velvet jewelled with thousands of twinkling stars. Below them sprawled the city in a vast panorama of rooftops and chimneys, and beyond the city lay the mountains, their black peaks silhouetted against the night sky. They were sitting on top of the wide, wide world.

The poor little shepherdess had never imagined anything so big. It made her feel small and helpless, and very very frightened. She hid her face in the chimney sweep's breast and wept bitterly.

"The world is too large," she sobbed. "I see now that I could never be happy here. If you love me, please take me back home to the table under the looking glass."

The unhappy sweep tried to reason with her. "If we go back," he said, "you will have to marry the Goatsleg High Adjutant Sergeant-Major. Surely you cannot want that."

But even the thought of the angry old Chinese mandarin and her ugly suitor did not deter the little shepherdess, and nothing the sweep said could make her change her mind. She pleaded with him so tearfully and looked with such horror on the panorama below them that at last he agreed to take her back, though it seemed a foolish idea to him.

So they climbed back down the dark chimney, and as there was no star to guide them this time the journey was even more difficult than before. Several times the little shepherdess missed her footing, and had the sweep not caught her in time she would have fallen to the hearth below and broken into little pieces.

As for the sweep, his heart was heavy, for he knew that once they returned to the mandarin he would lose his sweetheart to the Goatsleg High Adjutant Sergeant-Major. She would be shut up in the black cabinet and he would never see her again.

At last they reached the bottom of the chimney, and after listening to satisfy themselves that all was quiet in the room they stepped out.

A terrible sight greeted them. There on the floor lay the Chinese mandarin, broken into three pieces; his back had come away in one piece and his head had rolled into the corner of the room. He had fallen off the table in an attempt to follow the runaways.

"Oh, this is terrible," exclaimed the shepherdess. "My old grandfather is broken into pieces and it is all our fault. I will never forgive myself, never."

"He can be put together again," the chimney sweep reassured her. "If they glue his back together and put a strong rivet in his neck he will be as good as new again, and probably just as unpleasant and overbearing too."

And that is exactly what happened. The mandarin was repaired, and he was in every way as good as new again, except that, owing to the rivet in his neck, he could not nod his head.

"Have I your permission to wed your grand-daughter?" asked the Goatsleg High Adjutant Sergeant-Major, when the mandarin was back in position on the table.

The shepherdess and the chimney sweep held their breath in agony, for fear that the old man might nod his head. But nod he could not, and he was too proud to admit to a stranger that he had a rivet in the back of his neck.

So the young couple remained together on the table under the looking glass, blessing the mandarin's rivet and loving each other until they were eventually broken.

The Hare and the Tortoise

The Hare was always boasting how fast he could run, and never a day passed without him challenging the other animals to a race.

No animal would accept the challenge until one day a small voice said, "I will race you."

The Hare roared with laughter. "You, Tortoise?" he mocked. "Why, I can beat you in a few minutes."

"Can you indeed?" replied the Tortoise quietly. "We shall see. Let the race begin."

The signal to start was given and the Hare quickly ran on ahead, with the Tortoise crawling much more slowly behind him.

The Hare was so confident that he would win that he decided to have a nap in the warm sun.

Meanwhile, the Tortoise plodded on and on until he passed the Hare, who was still fast asleep.

The Hare awoke just in time to see the Tortoise crawling over the finishing line, to the warm applause of his animal friends.

The Hare bounded along . . . but he was too late, the Tortoise had won.

"You see, you should never be too confident," said the Tortoise with a smile at the angry Hare. "I may be slow and steady, but I have won the race."

The Fox and the Stork

The Fox and the Stork were once very good friends and they visited each other often.

But one day the Fox played a very spiteful joke on the Stork. He invited the Stork to dinner and the Stork accepted the invitation happily.

But when the Stork arrived, she found that the dinner consisted of soup, served in a very shallow bowl. Because of her long bill, the Stork was unable to drink the soup, and she was forced to sit there, hungry, while the sly Fox easily ate the soup from both the shallow bowls.

"I am sorry that you did not like my soup," he chuckled, as he lapped up the last drop.

"Oh, pray do not apologise," replied the Stork. "Come tomorrow night and have dinner with me."

The greedy Fox accepted the Stork's invitation eagerly, but when he arrived, he found *his* soup was served in a tall, narrow jar!

He was very angry as he watched the Stork enjoying her soup, while he could only lick the drops which had gathered outside the jar.

But the Stork laughed as she said, "I am not going to apologise to you, friend Fox. I am just going to say that unless you are able to take a joke, you should never play tricks on others."

The Twelve Dancing Princesses

Once upon a time, in the days when princesses were more plentiful than they are now, there was a king with twelve daughters. Each princess was very beautiful, as princesses should be, and they lived an idle, luxurious life in the Royal Palace, sleeping late every morning, and eating breakfast in bed every day and not just on Sundays.

But there was a mystery surrounding the twelve princesses. As the king was a very possessive father he made sure that every night, when the princesses were safely tucked up in their golden beds, the great door to their bedroom was securely bolted. And yet, in the morning, the princesses' satin slippers were always worn into holes.

When asked what they had been doing all night, the princesses would yawn and say, "Why, sleeping, of course." But this answer only deepened the mystery of the worn slippers.

The king grew more and more puzzled, and at last he decided to issue a proclamation saying that any man who could solve the mystery of the worn slippers would earn a large reward and the hand of one of the princesses in marriage.

The proclamation went out, and it wasn't long before the first prince arrived. He was given three days and three nights in which to solve the mystery, and on the first night he waited confidently outside the princesses' room. However, when morning came he was found fast asleep at the foot of the door, and once again the princesses' satin slippers were worn into holes.

On the second and third nights the prince fared no better. He was sent away in disgrace, and told never to return.

Over the next few months a further ten princes tried to solve the mystery of the twelve princesses, but each one failed miserably and was banished from the kingdom. The king was in despair, and he promised even greater riches than before to anyone who could tell him how his daughters could wear out their shoes without ever leaving their room.

At about this time a young soldier who had been wounded in battle was returning home. Hearing the king's proclamation he decided to take a detour and try his luck. He set off through the forest, and on his way he almost fell over a pig as it charged through the undergrowth. A little further on he met an old woman in tears, bewailing the loss of her one and only pig.

"I was taking him to market," she sobbed, "but now he's run away. What shall I do?"

The kind young soldier immediately set off after the pig, and in spite of his wound he soon caught up with it and returned it to the old woman.

"Thank you, young man," she said, wiping her eyes on her apron. "You have done me a good turn and I would like to repay you if I can."

"Then perhaps you can tell me how the king's daughters wear out their slippers every night," said the soldier.

"I can't tell you that," replied the old woman, "but I can give you this." She handed him an old cloak. "It will make you invisible, but you must remember not to drink the wine that one of the princesses will bring you. Good luck, young man."

The soldier thanked her and, taking the magic cloak, he set off for the Royal Palace.

The king was not very impressed when he saw the soldier's shabby clothes, and at first refused to consider him as a candidate. However, it was some time since the last prince had failed, and the king was anxious to have the mystery solved, so at last he relented and agreed to give the soldier a chance.

"You have three days and three nights," he said, "and if you fail I shall have your ears cut off for your impertinence."

The soldier bowed low, and clutched his magic cloak tightly. That night he waited until the twelve princesses had gone to bed, then he positioned himself outside their door, with the cloak hidden under his coat.

He hadn't been there long when the youngest princess came out and offered him a goblet of wine. The soldier accepted the wine and bowed humbly as the princess returned to the bedroom.

The soldier was so overcome by the princess's beauty that he almost forgot the old woman's warning and raised the goblet of wine to his lips. But, just in time, he remembered, and he quickly tipped the wine into a nearby urn.

Then he tied the magic cloak round his shoulders, and immediately he became invisible. He slipped into the princesses' room to find them all dressed in their finest gowns, their new satin slippers peeping out from under their skirts. The soldier had never seen so many beautiful women, and yet he still thought that the youngest princess was the loveliest of all.

"Is it safe to go?" asked the eldest princess.

"Oh, yes," laughed the youngest princess, whose name was Sophie. "We won't have any trouble from that shabby fellow. Let's go at once."

Although he was invisible, the soldier felt his cheeks grow crimson at her cruel words, and he resolved to win her love at all cost.

The eldest princess touched a carving on one of the great gold beds and before the astonished soldier's eyes a trapdoor slid open by his feet. He stepped back quickly as one by one the princesses began to descend the flight of stairs.

Princess Sophie was the last to go, and in his haste the soldier trod on her gown as she stepped down. "Oh! Someone is holding my dress!" she cried in alarm.

"Nonsense," chided the sister in front of her. "You have probably caught it on a nail, that is all."

The soldier gave a sigh of relief and followed the princesses as they descended the secret stairway. Down they went, deeper and deeper, until at last they emerged in a brightly-lit grotto.

They set off down a path lined with trees which had leaves of gold and silver. Eventually they came to a lake. On the lake were twelve boats made of crystal, and in each boat was a fairy prince, waiting to row the princess across the water.

One by one the boats set off, and the soldier stepped into the last boat with the youngest princess. As they pulled away from the shore the fairy prince remarked that the boat seemed heavier than usual, but Princess Sophie said that it was probably the heat that was making him feel drowsy.

As they crossed the water the sound of music drifted out to them from a wonderful castle on the far shore, its walls built entirely of crystal, and lamps gleaming from every room. A fairy ball was in progress, and as the boats touched the shore, each prince led his princess up the crystal stairway to the ballroom.

The twelve princesses danced all night long to the sound of the fairy music, and as a crowing cock announced the approaching dawn, they finally sat down to supper, their slippers quite worn out.

The soldier had been watching the dancing, and although the princesses were all graceful dancers, to his mind the youngest princess far outshone her sisters.

As the pale light of dawn crept over the horizon, the fairy princes rowed back across the lake, and the princesses set off through the glittering trees, back to the palace. As he passed a silver tree, the soldier broke off one of the branches, as proof of his story.

"Oh! What was that noise?" cried Princess Sophie.

"It was nothing," said the eldest princess. "Just an owl hooting on one of the turrets."

They climbed the secret stairway back to their room, and the soldier quietly slipped out.

Like the twelve princesses, he slept for most of the day, but as night darkened the sky he positioned himself once again outside the princesses' bedroom, and waited.

Before long the youngest princess came out with a goblet of wine as before, and the soldier bowed low as she returned to the bedroom. Once again he poured the drugged wine into an urn and, slipping on the magic cloak, he followed the twelve princesses down the secret stairway into the grotto.

Once again he stepped into the crystal boat behind Princess Sophie, and as they set off it was she who remarked on the slow progress they were making. "It must be the heat," said the fairy prince, and he rowed harder, across the lake to the glittering castle.

The twelve princesses danced until dawn, and the young soldier watched as before. Then he rode across the lake in the crystal boat, and followed the princesses along the tree-lined path through the grotto.

As he passed a golden tree, he broke off one of the branches, and the youngest princess whirled round. "What was that noise?" she gasped.

"It was nothing," said the eldest princess. "Just an owl hooting in the trees."

The next morning, the princesses slept late as usual, but the soldier was busy. He felt ashamed of his shabby clothes, so he spent the day washing, ironing and mending his one and only suit of clothes in the hope that Princess Sophie would look more kindly on him.

That night, he took up his position as before.

Princess Sophie brought him the goblet of wine as usual, and as she gave it to him she noticed for the first time how handsome the soldier was. "What a pity it is that he will have his ears cut off," she thought to herself. Then she shrugged her shoulders and closed the heavy door behind her.

As she put on her best gown the princess felt a sudden draught, as if someone had come into the room, although when she looked there was no one there. "I feel uneasy," she told her sisters. "Perhaps we ought not to go tonight."

"What nonsense!" exclaimed the other princesses. "What could possibly happen? Come, let us go, the princes will be waiting."

The trapdoor slid open, revealing the flight of stairs, and they stepped daintily down, followed by the soldier.

The twelve princesses skipped along the path to the lake, eager to get to the ball, and the soldier had to hurry to keep up with them. When they reached the fairy castle, the princesses joined the dancers in the ballroom, and the invisible soldier settled down to watch.

But Princess Sophie was still uneasy, and every so often she would stop and look sadly around her, as she was seeing it all for the very last time.

"How restless you are tonight," teased one of her sisters, so the youngest princess smiled and pushed her suspicions from her mind as she returned to the dance.

As dawn approached, the dancing finally stopped and everyone sat down to a magnificent feast. The soldier waited until they had finished eating and drinking, and then he took one of the crystal goblets and hid it under his magic cloak.

67

The princesses were tired after dancing all night, and they walked slowly back through the grotto, but the soldier hurried on ahead and reached the secret stairway before them. When they reached their room, the other princesses fell exhausted onto their golden beds, but Princess Sophie tiptoed to the door and peeped round.

There was the soldier, fast asleep in the corner.

The princess was puzzled, but she told herself not to be silly, and she was soon fast asleep.

Meanwhile, the soldier, who had only been pretending to be asleep, had unwrapped the fairy goblet from his cloak and then he took from their hiding place the silver twig and the golden twig.

He went to see the king, taking these three things with him, and he told how the princesses spent every night dancing in a fairy castle. At first the king did not believe him, but the soldier produced the silver and gold twigs and the crystal goblet as proof of his story.

The king would have sent for the twelve
princesses at once, but the soldier said that it
would be kinder to let them sleep on a little
longer as they had been up all night. Also, he told
the king, he felt that he was not properly dressed
and would be very grateful if the king would lend
him a smarter suit of clothes.

"Of course," cried the king, and he sent for the
Royal Tailor to make a fine suit for the soldier.

At last the princesses were sent for, and the
king told them sternly that he knew their secret,
and from now on there would be no more fairy
balls and no more dancing till dawn. He then told
them that the young soldier had discovered their
secret and as a reward was going to choose one of
them as his wife.

Although he knew exactly which princess he would choose, the soldier walked along the line of princesses, bowing to each one, and he pretended to have great difficulty in making up his mind. At the end of the line, the youngest princess tried not to look concerned, although in her heart she longed for him to choose her.

At last, the soldier turned to the king and said, "I have made my choice. I wish to marry the Princess Sophie."

And marry her he did, with great pomp and ceremony. The king made him a prince, as befitted the husband of a princess, and you can be sure that they lived very happily.

As for the other princesses, their story too had a happy ending, for the eleven princes who had failed to solve the mystery were allowed to return to woo them, and soon they were all happily married.

The Boy who cried Wolf

There was once a boy whose task it was to look after a flock of sheep in some meadows just outside a village. But his was a lonely life, and one day, in order to get some attention, he rushed into the village crying: "Wolf! Wolf! A wolf is attacking my flock!"

Hearing his cries for help the villagers came with stout cudgels to ward off the wolf. But when they got to the meadows the sheep were contentedly munching the grass, safe from any harm.

The boy thought this was a good trick to play, and a few days later he cried "Wolf!" again, and once again the villagers came to his aid ... but all in vain.

But one day a wolf really did attack the flock and the boy cried "Wolf!" in earnest.

The villagers heard his cries but they thought that the boy was up to his tricks again and they did not come to help him. And so the poor sheep were set upon by the fierce wolf and killed!

So remember, never tell lies, because eventually a person who tells lies will never be believed ... even when he is really telling the truth!

The Fox and the Crow

One day an old Crow spied a piece of cheese on the table in a cottage, and in a trice she flew in at the open window, seized the cheese and flew away with it to the top of a tall tree.

A wily Fox who had seen all that had happened decided that the cheese would make a tasty supper for himself. So he decided to try and get the cheese from the Crow.

"Good morning, Madam Crow," he called. "How lovely you are looking today. Your feathers gleam like rich black silk in the sunlight, and your neck is more graceful than that of any swan, while your wings look stronger than those of the mighty eagle. And I am sure that your song is sweeter than that of the nightingale!"

The Crow was so flattered at this praise that she decided to show the Fox just how sweetly she could sing. She opened her mouth to caw . . . and down fell the cheese, into the Fox's waiting paws.

"Thank you for the cheese!" cried the Fox. "But next time, Madam Crow, do not be fooled by flattery. A person may be flattering you to serve his own purpose!"

HANSEL and GRETEL

Once upon a time, in a tumble-down old thatched cottage near a great, dark forest, lived a poor woodcutter and his family. They were happy together when times were good, but it seemed that no one wanted the wood that the woodcutter had to sell anymore, and so they were often hungry, and worried about the future.

One night the woodcutter went to open the old money-box on the mantelshelf and found nothing but a single gold coin. This was all the money they had left in the world.

"What are we to do?" the poor woodcutter asked his wife in despair. "This is surely the end of us!"

The woman sighed and a tear rolled down her cheek. "We are old," she replied. "We shall manage as we have done all these years. But what about little Hansel and Gretel, our dear children? What is to become of them?"

The husband and wife talked late into the night, trying to decide what to do for the best. And although they thought that the children were asleep, Hansel and Gretel were lying awake in the bed listening to everything that was said.

At last Hansel and Gretel heard their father say sadly: "I think we must send them away, although it will break our hearts. We shall give them our last coin, and some bread and cheese, and take them with us when we go cutting wood in the forest tomorrow. We shall leave them to rest and tell them that we shall return for them when we are finished, but we shall go back home instead. Perhaps the world will be kinder to them than we can be."

"Oh, husband, couldn't we keep them with us?" the mother cried. But the wood-cutter's mind was made up.

Lying in the darkness, Hansel and Gretel had heard every word and they were both very frightened.

"Oh, what shall we do?" Hansel said. But Gretel had an idea.

"Don't worry, brother," she told him, slipping from the bed and pulling on her jacket. "I know a way out."

And Gretel slipped out of the cottage into the garden, where the moonlight shone on several smooth pebbles lying on the path. She picked up as many pebbles as she could and put them in her pockets. Then she went back to bed.

The next morning the family awoke very early, and set off into the forest. They had not gone very far when Gretel stopped and turned around.

"Come along, Gretel!" called her father.

"I'm coming, Father. I am just looking at my pet dove sitting on the cottage roof," Gretel replied.

The woodcutter looked, too. "That's not your dove!" he said. "It's just the sunlight. Now do come on!"

But Gretel had really stopped to throw down one of her glistening pebbles. She stopped many times on the way into the dark forest to leave a trail of pebbles, so that Hansel and herself could find the way home themselves.

At last they reached a clearing where the woodcutter's tiny hut stood. Hansel and Gretel were told to stay there and rest, while their parents worked nearby chopping wood. They were given the bread, cheese and the gold coin, and then left quite alone in the silence of the huge forest.

After eating their food, they lay down to sleep. When they awoke it was quite dark. Holding hands, they took courage and went out to look for the pebbles.

There they were, shining as clear as could be in the moonlight. It was easy to follow them all the way home to the tumbledown thatched cottage.

How overjoyed and relieved the parents were to see Hansel and Gretel back, safe and sound! They had bitterly regretted what they had done, and told themselves that their luck would change and they would manage somehow.

For a while, things did seem to be better. They were all very happy. But then, one dark night, a thief stole all that they had, and they were in terrible distress. All that was left was a stale loaf of bread.

"We shall starve!" the woman cried. "Oh, what bitter misfortune!"

The husband wrung his hands. "Better for us to starve than dear Hansel and Gretel," he said. "Give the children the bread to eat for themselves, and we'll leave them in the forest once again, to find their own fortune. Perhaps a passing traveller will take pity on them and give them a home." Reluctantly, the woman agreed.

Now Hansel had been standing by the open window, and had heard every word spoken. His heart sank when he knew what was going to befall himself and his sister. He told Gretel that evening, and they wondered what they could do. "Never mind, Gretel," Hansel said at last. "I have an idea."

The next morning the family set out very early for the dark forest. When they reached the woodcutter's hut, the mother said goodbye. "Wait here like good children until we return for you," she told them, tears in her eyes.

Once again Hansel and Gretel fell asleep. When they woke they were hungry, and Gretel asked Hansel for a crumb of bread. But Hansel said he had none of the bread left, and led her by the hand to the edge of the clearing.

"I left a trail of breadcrumbs on the pathway here," he told his sister. "We shall make our way home if we follow them."

But there were no breadcrumbs lying in the forest. The woodland birds had eaten them all! So Hansel and Gretel wandered through the forest until they were completely lost.

Just as dawn was breaking they came upon another clearing in the trees, and saw the most beautiful little cottage standing there all alone. Going closer, they couldn't believe their eyes! The cottage was made of gingerbread, sweet and moist! The windows were of spun sugar, clear as the finest glass, and the roof was made of peppermint ice! The snow settled on the roof was creamy icing, and the walls were decorated with raisins and all kinds of sweets!

Hansel and Gretel couldn't believe their eyes. They were so hungry they ran up to the cottage and broke off pieces of it to eat. How delicious it tasted! They were so happy.

Just then a very old woman came out from the doorway and peered shortsightedly at them.

"What are you doing, eating up my little house?" she asked in a
cracked voice. Hansel and Gretel were very frightened.

"We are so hungry," Gretel said, "we didn't think –"

The old woman smiled. "You must come inside, then," she said.
"I always make hungry little children very welcome!"

So she took them each by the hand and led them inside her cottage.
It looked as cosy and comfortable as could be. There on the table was a
big plate of steaming hot pancakes covered in honey, and there was a
jug of hot milk, too.

"Eat, my dears," the old woman told them kindly. "Then when you
are sleepy, go to bed. I have made your beds ready." She pointed to
two little beds in the corner, made with fresh linen.

Hansel and Gretel could not believe their luck, and they ate their meal hungrily. Then they fell asleep in their beds to dream happy dreams of warmth and comfort.

But very early the next morning the dreams were shattered. Hansel had a terrible shock as the old woman dragged him from his bed and locked him into a cage with iron bars. For the old woman's kindness was really a trick: she was a wicked witch who liked to eat little children!

Cackling with glee, she slipped the key to Hansel's cage into her apron pocket. "There!" she said. "When I have fattened you up, you shall make me a tasty feast in my old age!"

Now she woke Gretel, pulling her from bed, too. "Get up!" she screeched. "I won't have you idling when there's work to be done!"

So poor Gretel was made to sweep, and scour, and polish, and do all kinds of chores for the old witch, the whole day long. And she was forced to prepare delicious, fattening meals for Hansel, while she herself was allowed only crumbs and crusts.

Each day the witch would test if Hansel was fat enough for eating yet by making him stick his finger through the bars of his cage. Hansel, knowing how shortsighted she was, stuck an old bone out for her to touch, instead of his own finger.

"You are eating all my food up, yet you're still as thin as a bone!" the old woman would shout as she touched the bone Hansel gave her.

But at last she lost patience and decided she would cook Hansel that very day. Now it seemed all hope was gone, and the children began to cry in despair.

But the hard-hearted witch ignored them and said to Gretel: "Come here and tell me if this oven is properly lit, child!"

Then Gretel had an idea. She went over to the stove and opened the door wide. Inside the stove the flames jumped high and hot.

"Oh, I can't see!" she cried all of a sudden. "A cinder has jumped into my eye!"

"Foolish girl!" the witch said crossly. "I suppose I shall have to look for myself!" And she bent down to peer in at the stove.

As soon as the old witch had bent down, Gretel pushed her as hard as she could into the stove – and slammed the door shut! But not before she had whisked the key to Hansel's prison from her apron pocket!

"Well done, my clever sister!" Hansel cried, overcome with joy to be freed. "And now Old Mother Witch will never harm anyone again!"

They found a great deal of treasure and gold in the old woman's cottage, and they collected as much as they could carry with them, leaving the rest for others to find. They took with them some food and drink, then they ran away from the magical gingerbread cottage.

For a while they walked through the tall, silent trees, searching for a familiar pathway between the dark shadows of the great forest. But no matter how far they walked they came to no pathway and saw no one to direct them which way they could go.

"Oh, to have survived such an adventure as being captured by a witch, only to wander aimlessly like this through the forest, with no hope of being saved or finding our way home seems so cruel!" Gretel wept, as they went on and on, often stumbling on the wicked briars which stood in their way.

At last darkness fell, and they settled down under the shelter of a great oak tree for the night. An owl hooted far above them, and they were very afraid, for the forest was a fearful place after darkness fell. But a silver moon rose above the trees, and they fell asleep at last, calmed by the gentle glow.

For many days they travelled in the great forest without seeing another living soul. Soon the food they had brought from the witch's cottage was all gone, and they survived by eating nuts and fruits from the trees.

One evening they lay down to sleep, but were wakened by the sweet singing of a white dove, sitting in the tall tree above them. They listened spellbound to the song which made them forget their troubles.

"Look!" cried Hansel. "I think the dove wants us to follow!" And the two children watched as the dove circled overhead, looking down on them with bright eyes. As they scrambled to their feet it flapped its wings and flew slowly away.

So Hansel and Gretel followed the white dove through the forest on a long, long journey. The dove watched over them and sat in the trees above, shining white as a star among the dark forest, while they slept at the end of each day.

At last the dove led them to the edge of the forest, and soon came to rest on the thatched roof of the woodcutter's cottage, beside its mate, Gretel's own white dove.

And there, chopping wood outside, was their father, and their mother was hanging out washing,

"Father! Mother!" Hansel and Gretel shouted, running towards them with arms outstretched.

The father swung his children high in the air and the mother hugged them, crying tears of joy that they were home safe and sound once more. For both parents had been heartbroken when they had heard no news of their children, despite their searching every day in the forest for word. And now here they were – come back to the cottage, rosy-cheeked and well!

Hansel and Gretel told the woodcutter and his wife all about their adventures, and they gave them the gold they had collected from the old woman's cottage. There was enough to make sure that the family would never be hungry again, and would be able to live in quiet comfort all their lives.

The woodcutter mended the tumbledown old cottage, and soon it was as spick-and-span as could be. The snow-white dove which had led Hansel and Gretel back home was rewarded with loving care, and so the mother, and the father, and Hansel and Gretel lived happily ever after in the little thatched cottage near the great, dark forest, and no misfortunes ever came near them again.

The Brave Little Tailor

One bright summer's morning a tailor sat cross-legged on his bench by the window, sewing a pair of trousers and whistling a cheerful tune. Presently a country woman passed his window crying, "Who'll buy my fine jams! Fine jams for sale!"

Now the tailor had that very morning bought a fresh crusty loaf, and he had a fancy for jam and bread, so he called the woman to the window and bought a pot of the jam. He cut a slice of the bread and spread it thickly with the jam. Then he put it on one side, saying to himself, "I'll just finish these trousers and then I can settle down to enjoy my lunch."

But while he was sewing, a hoard of flies, attracted by the smell of the jam, clustered on the slice of bread.

With a cry of rage, the tailor picked up a piece of material and struck out at the flies. Most of them flew away, but the tailor's aim was good, and when he counted he found that he had killed seven flies.

"What a brave fellow you are!" he said to himself. "The whole town must know of this deed." The tailor cut himself a belt of cloth, and on it he stitched the words: SEVEN AT ONE BLOW. As he fastened the belt round his waist, the tailor said, "Not only the town, but the whole world shall know of this."

Before he left, he looked around for something to take with him, but all he could find was a piece of stale cheese and a bird trapped in a bush beside the door. These he pushed into his pockets, and with a merry whistle he set off on his journey.

The tailor took the road that led up a mountain, for he was an active fellow and rarely felt tired. When he got to the top he found a great giant sitting by the roadside.

"Good morning to you," he said boldly. "I am on my way to seek my fortune. Would you care to come with me?"

The giant flung back his head and gave a great roar of scornful laughter. "You!" he said. "You are nothing but a miserable, good-for-nothing wretch, and I won't waste my time with you."

"As to that," said the tailor, not in the least put out, "you can see for yourself what kind of man I am." And he opened his coat to show the giant his belt.

When the giant read the words on the belt he thought that it was seven men the tailor had killed, and he felt more respect for the little man. However, he decided to test him, and picking up a pebble he squeezed it so hard that water dripped from it.

"There!" he said. "Do better than that if you can."

"Poof! Is that all?" said the tailor. "A child could do as well as that." He put his hand in his pocket and pulled out the piece of cheese. Then he squeezed it until the whey ran out.

The giant, who was rather short-sighted, thought that the tailor had squeezed a stone, and he was impressed that such a little man could be so strong. He picked up another pebble, and this time he flung it so far into the air that it disappeared for some time before returning to earth.

The tailor snorted. "That was quite a trick, but your pebble fell to the ground. My pebble will not fall." He put his hand into his pocket and drew out the bird. As he threw it into the air, the bird, glad to be free, flew straight up and did not come back.

"I must admit that you throw very well," said the giant. "Let's see how you are at carrying." He took the tailor to a large oak tree that had been cut down. "If you are as strong as you claim, help me carry this tree out of the forest."

"Of course," said the tailor, "*You* carry the trunk, and I will take the heavier twigs and branches."

The giant picked up the tree trunk and set it on his shoulder, while the cunning tailor, hidden by the rest of the tree, sat on the branches.

The giant, who was carrying both the tree and the tailor, soon became weary, and he called out, "I can't go on! I must put the tree down!" Quickly the tailor jumped down and grabbed the tree with both arms, as if he had been carrying it.

"What, a great fellow like you, and you can't even carry a tree?" he said.

They continued on their way, and came to a cherry tree, laden with fruit. The giant seized the top of the tree, where the ripest fruit hung, and gave it to the tailor to hold. But the tailor was not strong enough to hold the tree down, and as soon as the giant let go the tree sprang back into the air, taking the tailor with it.

As he landed on the other side, the giant said, "Are you so weak that you can't even hold down a bush like that?"

"Not at all," said the quick-witted tailor. "I was simply leaping out of the way of some stray shots from huntsmen in the forest. Jump after me if you can."

94

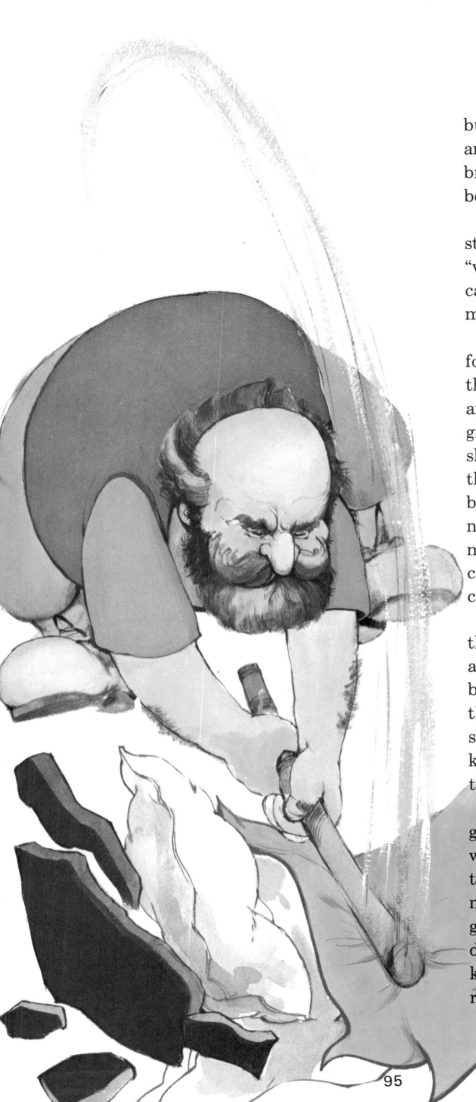

The giant gave a mighty leap, but he failed to clear the tree and caught his leg in the branches. The tailor had got the better of him again.

"Since you are such a brave, strong fellow," said the giant, "why don't you come back to my cave and spend the night with me and my two brothers?"

The tailor agreed, and he followed the giant to the cave. In the middle of the cave was a fire, and by the fire sat two huge giants, each with a roasted sheep in his hand. After supper, the giant showed the tailor to a bed where he could sleep for the night. However, the bed was much too big for the tailor, so he crept out of it and lay down in a corner.

After a while, when he thought the tailor would be asleep, the giant took an iron bar and beat the bed so hard that soon the blankets were in shreds. Thinking that he had killed the little tailor, the giant then went to bed.

In the morning, the three giants set out for the forest, but who should they meet but the tailor, whistling cheerfully as if nothing had happened. The giants were very frightened, and dreading that the tailor would kill them all with one blow they ran away as fast as they could.

The tailor travelled on alone, and after some time he entered the courtyard of a royal palace. He was tired after coming so far, so he lay down on the ground and went to sleep. As he lay there, people came to look at him, and they read the words on his belt: SEVEN AT ONE BLOW.

"Ah," they said, "this must be a great warrior to have killed so many with one blow." So they went and told the king.

The king thought that such a fighter would be very useful if war broke out, so he sent a courtier to beg for the tailor's services as soon as he woke up.

The courtier waited patiently until the tailor woke and stretched his limbs, and then he repeated the king's message. "That is the very reason why I came here," said the tailor, who by now was convinced of his own bravery and had forgotten that his victims had only been flies.

He was taken to the king and honours were heaped on him.

However, the king's generals were jealous of the little tailor and they wished him at the other end of the world. They talked among themselves and at last they went to the king and told him that unless he got rid of the tailor they would have to resign.

Now the king was sorry that his old and faithful generals should wish to leave him, and he wished he had never seen the stranger. However, he was afraid to dismiss him, as he feared that the tailor would kill him and his subjects and take over the throne.

He thought for some time, and at last he came up with a plan. Sending for the tailor he said, "I have a favour to ask of so great a warrior as yourself. In my kingdom there are two giants who have committed many murders and robberies, and burnt much property. None of my subjects dare go near them for fear of their lives. If you can overcome them I will reward you with half my kingdom and will give you my only daughter in marriage."

"Well, well," thought the tailor, "here is a job for me. It is not every day that I am offered a king's daughter and half a kingdom." To the king he said, "I will soon conquer those two giants. What are they to a man who has killed seven at one blow!"

The king sent a hundred knights with the tailor. But as he approached the forest where the giants lived, the tailor said, "You stay here. I prefer to meet the giants alone." He crept into the forest, and after searching he found the giants asleep under a tree.

Filling his pockets with stones, the tailor climbed nimbly up the tree and crawled along a branch until he lay above one of the sleeping giants. He took a handful of stones and let them fall, one after the other, onto the giant's chest.

At last the giant woke, and he turned to his companion saying, "Why are you hitting me?"

"You must have been dreaming," said the other. "I never touched you." They lay down again and were soon fast asleep.

The tailor then threw stones at the other giant, who woke with a start and said angrily, "Don't knock me about like that!"

"You are dreaming," said the first giant, and they argued for a while before falling asleep again. Up in the tree, the tailor took out a bigger stone, and dropped it on the first giant's chest. This was too much for the giant, and with an angry roar of pain he leapt on the other giant like a madman.

They fought hard, tearing up trees and beating each other until at last they both lay dead.

The tailor jumped down from his hiding place and stabbed each giant. Then he went back to the horsemen and said, "Well, I did it, but what a fight they put up! They later uprooted trees to defend themselves against me. But what is that to a man who has killed seven at one blow!"

The horsemen did not believe him, so the tailor showed them the scene, with the giants lying dead and uprooted trees all around them.

When the tailor returned, the king refused to give him the reward until he had performed another task. "In the forest lives a unicorn," said the king, "and it is causing great damage. Catch him for me and you shall have your reward."

"I fear the unicorn less than I did the giants," boasted the tailor.

He set off for the forest with a length of rope and an axe, and when he reached the outskirts he told the horsemen to wait there for his return. Then he went in search of the unicorn.

The fabulous creature soon appeared, and charged straight at the tailor. However, he leapt nimbly out of the way behind a tree, and the unicorn, who was going too fast to stop, collided with the tree, its horn stuck fast in the trunk.

It was then a simple matter for the tailor to tie up the unicorn and free its horn with his axe.

The king was not pleased to see the tailor return, so he set yet another task before he would allow the tailor to marry his daughter. "I would like you to capture the fierce boar which has destroyed much property," he said.

"That is a simple task," said the tailor, "for a man who has killed seven at one blow."

The king sent his huntsmen with the tailor and they set off in search of the boar. However, after a time, the tailor told the huntsmen that he would prefer to catch the boar alone, which caused great relief as they had all had dangerous experiences with the wild beast.

The tailor went on alone into the forest.

As soon as the boar saw him it charged, baring its teeth. But the tailor was too quick for it and, spotting a woodcutter's hut nearby, he ran in through the door, then leapt out of a window at the back.

The furious beast ran into the hut after him, and the tailor quickly ran round the hut and slammed the door shut, trapping the boar inside, for he was too heavy to leap out of the window.

The tailor called for the huntsmen, to prove that he really had caught the boar, and then he presented himself again before the king.

The wedding was celebrated with great magnificence, if little rejoicing, and the brave little tailor became a king.

One night, the young queen woke to hear her new husband talking in his sleep. "Must finish this waistcoat . . . sew these trousers . . ." he was saying as he tossed and turned.

The queen realised at once her husband's real occupation and she was horrified. A tailor was hardly fit to be a king!

The next morning she went to her father and told him everything, begging him to free her from such a common man.

The king comforted her, and told her not to worry. "Leave your door open tonight," he said. "My servants will wait outside until this tailor is asleep, and then they will bind him and tie him in a sack and take him away in a ship."

The queen was pleased with this plan, but her young page boy was loyal to the tailor and he told his master everything.

"Don't worry," said the tailor, "I will spoil their little plot."

That night they went to bed as usual, and when the queen thought her husband was asleep she crept out of bed and opened the door.

However, the tailor was only pretending to be asleep, and suddenly he began to cry in a loud voice, "Boy, make me a coat and stitch up these trousers or I will lay this yardstick across your back. I have killed seven with one blow, I have slain two giants, captured a unicorn and trapped a wild boar. Why should I be afraid of those who stand outside my room?"

At these words the servants ran away in terror, and no one ever dared to oppose the tailor again.

He remained a king, and after a time his wife grew to love him and they ruled wisely and well for many years.

The End of a Friendship

MANY years ago, the elephant and the tiger were the best of friends. But that was before they learned that betting, between friends, is a dangerous pastime.

It all began one morning as they walked together through the dense jungle. They were discussing all sorts of grave issues, for both the tiger and the elephant sat on the high council which, under the supreme authority of the lion, ruled the jungle. But today the friends' serious discussions were disturbed by a little monkey who was leaping through the branches above them, chattering all the while.

"Be quiet!" roared the tiger.

"Silence!" trumpeted the elephant.

But the little monkey took not the slightest notice.

The elephant lost patience. "We must teach this monkey manners," he said. "Let us frighten him so much that he falls down from the tree."

It was the tiger who suggested that they make a bet on it. "If I cannot do it, you may eat me up. And if you cannot do it, then I will eat you up."

"Agreed," said the elephant.

"Then you begin," said the tiger.

So the elephant began to behave as if he had lost his wits, circling round the tree in which the monkey was perched and trumpeting so loudly that the earth shook.

The monkey, terrified by the din, jumped from branch to branch. Yet he did not drop to the ground.

The elephant continued until his throat was hoarse.

"Now it's your turn," he gasped to the tiger. "But don't forget, he must actually drop to the ground."

The tiger began to growl, snarl, grunt and roar. Then he made as if to spring into the tree.

The monkey became so crazed with fear that he lost his grip on the branch and dropped to the ground, directly in front of the tiger.

"You have won," groaned the elephant. "But let me have a week in which to say good-bye to my family and settle my affairs."

The tiger agreed and the elephant went home. For seven days he did not eat, nor drink, nor sleep. All he did was trumpet and trumpet and trumpet. All the animals came to see what was the matter; but when they heard they shook their heads sadly and went away.

News travels fast in the jungle – almost as fast as the beat of a drum. Yet it was the seventh day before the musk deer heard about the sad affair.

He hurried to the elephant's home, where his friend was even now taking a tearful leave of his family.

"I would be very sorry to lose you, friend elephant," said the musk deer. "We must certainly think of some way to save you."

"If you only can," pleaded the elephant, "I shall be your servant for life and so shall all my relatives."

The clever little musk deer set to work quickly. Getting a big bottle of palm syrup he poured it over the elephant's back, letting the red syrup run down his sides and legs.

"Now I will ride on your back," said the musk deer. "And, as I am licking the syrup off your back, you must trumpet as loudly as you can and wriggle from side to side as though you were in terrible pain."

So they set off through the jungle, the elephant making as loud and as miserable a noise as if the musk deer was indeed eating him alive.

When they arrived at the meeting place the tiger was already there.

"A tiger!" exclaimed the musk deer, smacking his lips. "And a fat one too. That might satisfy my hunger better than this leathery old elephant."

Hearing these words and listening to the screams of the elephant, the tiger quickly fled.

Crashing through the underbrush he met the great black ape.

"Who's chasing you?" asked the ape. He was rather annoyed because, being slow-moving, he had been nearly knocked down by the tiger's onslaught.

"Oh, please do not delay me," gasped the tiger. "The most terrible creature is eating my dear friend the elephant, who should have been my supper tonight. And this creature threatened to eat me too. I must get home quickly!"

"Indeed," muttered the ape, half to himself. "This sounds just like my old school friend, the musk deer. He was always playing tricks – quite a clever little fellow for his size!"

The ape persuaded the tiger to go back with him into the jungle. "You need not be afraid, I will protect you," he promised the tiger.

Soon they met the musk deer, riding on the elephant's back and licking up the syrup.

But the musk deer was a quick thinker. "Hello, Uncle Ape," he shouted in greeting. "You've let me down, I see. You promised to bring me three tigers and all you've brought me is one, and an old one at that. I'll make a start with that, it will have to do for a first course."

Hearing this, the tiger turned tail and fled for his life. "Miserable rogue!" he roared back at the ape. "You tried to trick me so that your friend could have me for his supper. If ever you cross my path again I shall eat you myself."

The tiger ran into the jungle, and he probably hasn't stopped running yet. But from that day on the tiger and the ape have been deadly enemies.

The Goose Girl

There was once a Queen whose husband had been dead many years, but she had a daughter who, as well as being beautiful, was also kind and gentle. As a child the Princess had been betrothed to the son of a King of a faraway country, and now the time drew near for the marriage to take place.

The Queen packed her daughter's dowry with great care, for it included gold and jewels, silver trinkets and an exquisite wedding dress fit for a royal bride.

As the Queen loved her daughter dearly, she thought that the Princess might be lonely on the long journey to her new home, so she arranged for a maid to accompany the Princess.

She ordered two horses to be saddled and the dowry to be put in panniers on the side of one of the animals.

"I am entrusting your dowry to the maid for safekeeping," the Queen said to her daughter. "But you must ride Falada, my dear child, for he has the gift of human speech and he can both talk and understand what others say."

Before the Princess left, the Queen cut off a lock of her own hair and gave it to her daughter.

"Put this into the locket which you wear about your neck," she said. "It will act as a charm to keep you from any harm which might otherwise befall you along the way. I want you to reach your journey's end in safety."

"I will take great care of it, dear mother," cried the Princess. "Pray do not worry about me."

She put the charm into her locket. But, as her eyes were full of tears at the thought of the parting which was at hand, the Princess did not see that the catch was broken and the locket was not closed properly.

"Always remember that you are a Princess," cried her mother as she kissed her farewell. "Treat everyone kindly, return good for evil and in times of trouble never lose heart."

"I will remember," promised the Princess, and she and her maid set off on the long journey to her new home.

For a time all went well, but then the Princess began to notice that her maid was very short tempered with her royal mistress, and answered all conversation with a very bad grace.

When they came to a small brook the clear water made the Princess feel thirsty, and she said to her maid, "Pray get down from your horse and fill my golden cup with water from yonder brook, if you please."

"But I do not please!" retorted the maid haughtily. "I have waited on you long enough. If you want to drink, lean over the brook and cup the water in your own hands and drink."

The Princess was so thirsty that she did as the maid ordered.

But as she climbed onto her horse Falada again, she whispered, "Alas, what will become of me?"

And the lock of her mother's hair in the locket about her neck answered:

"Alas, alas, if thy mother knew it,
Sadly, sadly, her heart would rue it!"

But the Princess remembered her mother's words about how a Princess should behave, and so she said nothing about her maid's ill-behaviour and once again they set off on the journey.

The sun was hot, and as they rode it grew hotter and hotter, until the Princess needed to drink once more.

When they came to a river, the Princess asked her maid once more to get her a cup filled with water.

"Drink if you will," replied the maid, "but I will no longer serve you."

So the Princess leaned over the water to drink, saying sadly: "What will become of me?"

And once again the lock of hair answered:

"Alas, alas, if thy mother knew it,
Sadly, sadly, she would rue it!"

As the Princess started to drink, her locket flew open and the lock of hair floated away down the river.

The Princess did not notice that her charm had gone, but the spiteful maid saw it float away, and she smiled to herself. Now that the Princess had not got her mother's charm to protect her, the maid could put her wicked plans into action.

The Princess wiped her hands on a dainty handkerchief after quenching her thirst at the river, and then she walked over to where her faithful steed, Falada, stood waiting patiently.

But before the Princess could mount again, the maid seized the reins and pushed the Princess roughly to one side.

"It is time I had a fine horse to ride!" she cried. "And since it is fine clothes which make a Princess, I will wear your clothes and you shall wear mine and ride my horse too! Then you will know how it feels to be a serving maid and wait on others who are no better than you!"

The maid looked so fierce and spiteful that the Princess did not dare argue, and she meekly did as the maid ordered.

The maid threatened to kill the Princess if she told anyone what had taken place and, looking at her maid's wicked face, the Princess knew that the maid was capable of doing this if she dared to disobey her.

So, dressed in the maid's homespun clothes, the Princess mounted her servant's horse and rode meekly a few paces behind the maid who proudly sat upon Falada, preening herself in her new clothes.

But Falada knew all that had taken place, and although he did not speak his heart grieved for his own Princess. He saw how the Princess still acted with dignity as she remembered her mother's words, and he was very proud of his dear mistress.

At last the Princess and her wicked maid arrived at the royal court of her betrothed.

There was great joy and excitement at their arrival, and the young Prince, who had not seen the Princess for many years, rushed out into the courtyard to greet his bride.

He lifted the maiden who rode Falada down from her horse, scarcely giving her 'servant' a glance, and together they went inside the royal palace to see his father the King, leaving the real Princess alone in the courtyard.

But, unknown to them all, the King happened to be looking out of the window, and he saw the real Princess standing alone, talking sadly to Falada.

The King noticed what a sweet face she had and how, despite her homespun clothes, she had an air of dignity about her. He saw too that her tiny hands were soft and white as if they were unused to any rough work.

Just at that moment the Princess glanced up and she saw the kind old King looking at her. She longed to confide all her troubles to him, but she remembered her maid's cruel words. So instead, she dropped a shy curtsey, and hurried inside, looking for the servants' quarters in the royal palace.

The King was curious to know more about this gentle maiden, and when his son brought his bride to see him, he asked the maid Princess about the other girl.

The wicked maid was angry that the King should be interested in her servant, and she replied haughtily, "She is but a girl who accompanied me on my journey for company. But now that I have arrived here safely, pray give the girl some work to do, that she may not spend her days in idleness. Put her to work in the kitchens to scrub out the pots and pans."

But the King thought that this work was too rough for the young maiden who looked so gentle and kind, and after some thought he told the false Princess that her serving maid should help Curdken, the young lad who looked after the royal geese.

The false Princess clapped her hands in delight.

"Yes, yes, she shall be a goose girl!" she cried.

119

But later, when the false Princess was alone with the Prince, she began to worry in case Falada spoke to someone about what happened on the journey. She knew that Falada was a magic horse and could speak, and that he loved his royal mistress very dearly.

So she said coaxingly, "Dear Prince, will you do me a small kindness?"

"That I will gladly," replied the Prince, "if it is within my power and it will make you happy."

"Then pray have the horse upon which I rode here destroyed," she cried. "It is an unruly creature and tried to unseat me every step of the way. It is too dangerous a horse for anyone to ride."

The Prince was very sad to hear this request, for he had thought that Falada was a truly magnificent horse. But he wished to please his betrothed bride, and so he gave orders for the horse to be killed.

But when the real Princess heard of the fate which had befallen her poor horse, she went to the man who had performed the deed, and she begged him to put up Falada's head over the city gateway so that she might see it whenever she went past with the geese.

The man thought that this was a very strange request, but he liked the little Goose Girl with her gentle ways, and he did as she asked.

The next morning as Curkden and the Goose Girl passed through the city gates with their gaggle of geese, Falada's head looked down at them.

Looking up at her horse, the Goose Girl said sadly, "Falada, Falada, ours is a sad fate, I fear!"

And to Curkden's great amazement, the horse replied,

"Bride, bride, the true bride I hold dear,
Alas, alas! If thy mother knew it,
Sadly, sadly, her heart would rue it!"

With a last look at her horse, the Goose Girl followed Curkden and drove the geese out of the city towards the meadows beyond.

Once the geese were safely fenced off in the meadow, the Goose Girl sat down upon a bank and, taking the one treasure which still remained to her, a golden comb, she took the pins from her hair and began to comb her hair.

In the sunlight the Goose Girl's hair shone like pure silver, it was so beautiful and fair, Curkden thought it was so lovely that he tried to pull a lock of the girl's hair from her head so that he might keep it for himself.

But before he could do this, the Goose Girl cried:

"Blow, breezes, blow!
Let Curdken's hat go!
Blow, breezes, blow!
Let him after it go!
O'er hills and dales and rocks,
Away be it whirled,
Till the silvery locks
Are all combed and curled!"

And immediately a great wind blew Curkden's hat away, and off he had to go, chasing it over hill and dale until he caught it.

By the time Curdken had caught his hat, the Goose Girl had combed and pinned up her tresses once again, and it was time to take the geese back to the city.

The next morning, as they took the geese to the meadows again, the Goose Girl and her horse greeted each other in exactly the same way as before.

Once again the Goose Girl started to comb her hair, singing the same little rhyme . . . and once again Curdken had to run off to chase after his hat.

This time when he returned he was so cross with the Goose Girl that he resolved to tell the King all about it when he returned to the city that night.

The King listened to the lad's story, and then he told him to go out as usual the following day.

But early the next morning, before even Curdken was up, the King hid in the shadows of the city gate, and here he saw and heard the Goose Girl speak to her horse.

Then, while Curdken and the Goose Girl herded the geese through the gates, the King hurried to the meadow and hid behind a large bush.

The King saw the girl start to comb her hair and clearly over the sweet morning air came her little song:

"Blow, breezes, blow!
Let Curdken's hat go!
Blow, breezes, blow!
O'er hills, dales and rocks,
Away be it whirled,
Till the silvery locks
Are all combed and curled!"

The King watched in amazement and then he almost laughed out loud as the gooseherd went running after his hat. But his eyes grew thoughtful as he watched the Goose Girl combing her hair, and as a sulky and cross Curdken returned with his hat, the King slipped away, unseen by either of them.

That night as the little Goose Girl crept back to the palace, hoping to slip unnoticed into the stables where she slept on a bed of straw, she found the King awaiting her.

Gently the King told her of all he had seen that day, and he asked her to tell him what it was all about.

At this the Goose Girl grew pale with fear and she started to weep, remembering her cruel maid's words. But the King begged her to tell him, so that at last the Goose Girl told the King the whole story.

The King's face grew dark with anger as he listened, but at the end, he led the Goose Girl into the palace, and ordered a servant to bring her clothes fit for a princess.

Even the King was amazed at the Princess's beauty when she was arrayed in her beautiful gown. As for the young Prince, when he saw his true bride he fell in love at once, for secretly he had felt that the false Princess had a cruel heart.

Then the King ordered a great feast to take place to celebrate the forthcoming marriage of his son and his bride.

The King sat at the head of the table while the Prince sat between the false Princess and the Goose Girl, but none recognised the true Princess in her fine clothes, not even Curdken, who had been invited to the feast.

When they had all eaten, the King told them a story about a servant who had tricked and deceived her mistress.

"What should be done to anyone behaving thus?" said the King to the false Princess.

"Such a person should be banished from the Kingdom, and ordered never to return on pain of death!" replied the false princess.

"You have just pronounced your own punishment," cried the King sternly. "For you are such a maidservant!" And he told the royal court what she had done.

So the wicked maid was justly punished, and the Prince married his true Princess, and they lived together in peace and happiness all their lives.

The Fox and the Grapes

One day a Fox was walking through a vineyard when he saw a cluster of grapes hanging high up on a vine. It was a very hot day and the Fox had neither eaten nor drunk since the evening before, and the juicy grapes looked very tempting indeed.

"Those grapes look delicious!" he cried. "They will be both food and drink for me!" And he jumped up at the vine as high as he could.

But he could not reach the grapes! He tried again and again, but each time he failed to reach the juicy grapes.

At last he was forced to give up and, weary and worn out with his efforts, he slunk out of the vineyard.

"I never really wanted those grapes in the first place," he said to himself, as he gave the vine one last look. "I am not really hungry at all . . . and I am sure those grapes are sour!"

This little story only goes to prove that it is easy to pretend that what we can't get isn't worth having!

The Cat and the Mice

There was once a family of Mice who lived in a house where their lives were plagued by the antics of a very large Cat.

At last they decided to hold a council-of-war to decide the best way to deal with their enemy.

"I have the answer," said one cocky young Mouse. "We will tie a bell around the Cat's neck so that it will tinkle whenever she walks about. This way we will always know when the Cat is coming our way, and we will be able to hide and no longer go in fear of our lives!"

Everyone agreed that this was a splendid idea, and the answer to all their problems.

But an old Mouse, who had managed to live for a long time because he was wise in the ways of the world, said quietly, "It is a very fine idea. But which one of us is going to put the bell on the Cat?"

As all the other Mice grew silent, he added wisely, "It is easier to think of a plan than to carry it out!"

RAPUNZEL

Once upon a time there was a kindly couple who lived in a cottage near an enormous forest. The husband worked as a woodcarver, and they were very happy with each other, except for just one thing. They longed for a child, but no child came to them. So they lived alone, just the two of them, as the years passed by.

Now from the back window of their cottage the man and his wife could see a lovely garden behind a high brick wall. Growing in the garden were rows and rows of the richest vegetables, fruits and flowers you were ever likely to see, and tall trees growing on the lawn. It was a wonderful place and the woman could sit at her window and stare at it all day long. There was a stream flowing through it, and across the stream a pretty bridge arched, and birds sang and played there from dawn till dusk.

One day the wife looked out at the garden and she saw some fine cherries clustered on a cherry tree. A strange feeling came over her, and she yearned for those cherries all day. At last her husband noticed how pale and miserable she was, and he asked her what was the matter.

"Oh, dear," she replied, "I shall die unless I taste those cherries in the garden!"

The husband sighed. He knew the garden belonged to a wicked witch whom everyone feared. But when he saw how unhappy his wife was, he told her that he would climb into the garden that night and bring her the cherries.

So when darkness fell he climbed over the high wall and went to the cherry tree. Picking a cluster of the fruit, he hurried back and brought them to his wife.

She was overjoyed, and ate the cherries immediately. They were, she declared, the most delicious cherries she had ever tasted. The man sighed with relief, thinking that now she would be satisfied.

But the very next evening he found his wife once more sitting at the back window, yearning for another taste of the cherries which glistened on the tree over the wall.

He knew he would have no peace until once again he climbed into the witch's garden and stole the cherries. So that night, after dusk, he made his way into the garden with a pouch to hold the cherries.

131

But just as he was picking them from the branch, he heard a laugh behind him and he turned to see the witch staring at him with terrible, burning eyes.

He was terrified when she cried furiously: "How dare you steal my cherries, you thief! You shall pay for this!"

"Oh, please be kind," the man pleaded. "I only did it because my wife saw your garden from her window and yearned to taste these cherries! She said she would die if she could not have them!"

"Well," said the witch, "if that's true then you can take all the cherries you wish. But I make one condition."

"Anything, anything!" the man cried in distress.

The witch laughed once more. "You gave your word," she reminded him. "Well, your wife will have a child shortly – a girl with golden hair. I shall have her, and bring her up like my own!"

Then she disappeared in a cloud of smoke.

The man managed to return to his wife and they were filled with grief. Sure enough, a daughter was born to them, and the witch came to carry her away.

The girl, who was called Rapunzel, was
very beautiful. When she was grown up the
old witch shut her up in a lonely tower in
the very centre of the great forest. The
tower had no door, only a small window
right at the top. When the witch came to
see her, she would call:

"Rapunzel, Rapunzel,
Let down your golden hair."

And Rapunzel would let her long, long
braided hair fall out of the window so that
the witch could climb up on it to the room.
The witch came once every day, but for
the rest of the time Rapunzel was alone.
She would sit at the window and look out
at the forest and dream that she was free.
She was very unhappy in the tower, and she
disliked the old witch. She often longed to
be a bird so that she could fly away and
escape.

Many years passed, and at last Rapunzel thought that she would have to stay in the tower for the rest of her life. But then, one day, the king's son was riding in the forest when he heard the sweetest singing.

Trying to find its source, he came to the tower, and there he saw Rapunzel sitting at the window, singing to pass away the hours. The king's son fell in love with her at once. He couldn't forget the haunting sadness of her voice nor her lovely face.

But why was she shut up in such a strange tower? He couldn't understand it. He watched Rapunzel from a distance as she sat at the window, feeling the sunlight on her face and talking to the forest birds who came to perch on the windowsill. The king's son was moved with pity and love and he decided he would rescue her from her imprisonment.

The very next day he returned on his horse. But just as he was about to talk to Rapunzel, he heard someone approaching. He hid himself behind a great tree and waited.

It was the witch arriving, singing tunelessly to herself in a cracked old voice. When she came to the foot of the tower she raised her head and called:

"Rapunzel, Rapunzel,
Let down your golden hair."

Then the king's son saw Rapunzel let down her long golden plait from the window, and watched in amazement while the old witch climbed up. That very instant he decided he would do the same.

The next day, when it was evening, he rode through the forest to the lonely tower and cried in a loud voice:

"Rapunzel, Rapunzel,
Let down your golden hair!"

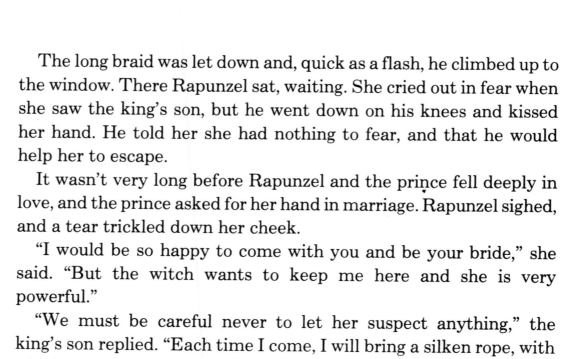

The long braid was let down and, quick as a flash, he climbed up to the window. There Rapunzel sat, waiting. She cried out in fear when she saw the king's son, but he went down on his knees and kissed her hand. He told her she had nothing to fear, and that he would help her to escape.

It wasn't very long before Rapunzel and the prince fell deeply in love, and the prince asked for her hand in marriage. Rapunzel sighed, and a tear trickled down her cheek.

"I would be so happy to come with you and be your bride," she said. "But the witch wants to keep me here and she is very powerful."

"We must be careful never to let her suspect anything," the king's son replied. "Each time I come, I will bring a silken rope, with which you must make a ladder. When the time comes you will escape on it and we will ride away together to the palace!"

So Rapunzel agreed, and for a while the prince visited Rapunzel each day after the witch had gone. Slowly but surely, Rapunzel's nimble fingers made the silken ladder until there remained only one more rope to be sewn.

That evening the prince came as usual and called:

"Rapunzel, Rapunzel,
Let down your golden hair."

But it so happened that the witch was coming back, having forgotten a book of spells she had left in the tower. She arrived at the tower just in time to see the prince climbing up the thick rope of Rapunzel's hair. She was beside herself with rage! Almost too furious to speak, she hurried away.

The king's son had brought the last rope for the ladder and Rapunzel was sewing it when the witch returned the next day. Rapunzel had a terrible shock when she heard the witch crying:

"Rapunzel, Rapunzel,
Let down your golden hair."

She had just time to hide the ladder before the witch climbed up.

"You're earlier than usual, Mother Witch," she said nervously.

"Wicked child!" the witch screeched in reply. "You have been deceiving me, haven't you?" She searched for the ladder and threw it from the window so that it was lost among the trees. Then in a fury she took some scissors and cut Rapunzel's long plait.

The witch took Rapunzel with her to an even lonelier place by the edge of the sea, where she would never be found. Then she hurried back to the forest, leaving Rapunzel weeping in despair.

She then returned to the tower and climbed up on the plait, which, as she cut it, she had hung from the window on a hook. She wound up the hair once more, then sat down and smiled when she heard:

"Rapunzel, Rapunzel,
Let down your golden hair."

She let down the plait slowly and soon the prince was climbing lithely upwards, his heart full of happiness because he meant that day to take Rapunzel away from the tower to the palace, where they would be married.

But he had a terrible shock when he reached the window and looked inside. Instead of seeing Rapunzel's dear face he saw the witch's hideous eyes peering at him from the shadows inside.

"So!" she shrieked at him. "Your Rapunzel is gone! I have taken her far away from you. You will never see her again - and I will claw your eyes out!" She reached out for him with her long nails, and in trying to avoid her, the king's son fell from the tower. He was hurt, but his life had been saved by falling on some bushes. They were covered with thorns which scratched at his eyes and blinded him. The cackling, cruel laughter of the witch echoed in his ears as he stumbled away.

Beside himself with grief and despair, the prince wandered for months in the great forest, speaking to no one. He kept himself alive by eating berries and nuts and drinking water from streams. Soon his clothes were torn and dirty and he was no longer a handsome young prince dressed in silk and gold. Finally he gave up all hope of ever seeing his dearest Rapunzel again, and he believed he would never return to his father's palace and the rich, happy life he had there. He was completely lost. Wandering for miles through endless forests, over steep hills and across dark valleys, he lost all knowledge of where he was, and didn't care. It was as if his life was over. He spent his days in misery, seeing nothing of the world around him, weeping and lamenting what had happened to him.

Meanwhile the king, who was desperately worried for his son, had sent troops of soldiers to search the country, and offered a large reward for any news of the missing prince. But although the soldiers looked in every village and every wood they found nothing. Once a band of soldiers on horseback passed the king's son on a lonely country road, thinking he was only a blind beggar.

Gradually, as the days passed, the king's son began to take more notice of the world, and of the many people who were kind to him. He was grateful for the food poor farmers gave him on his journey, and told himself that if ever he was restored to his position of power at the palace he would repay the peasants who had helped him.

Then one day he had come so far that he reached the edge of the sea. As he walked on the shore he felt the cold sea wind in his face. Knowing he could go no further, he was overcome with despair. Lying down on the sand he fell asleep. The prince slept for a long time, while the waves lapped close to him and the sun gradually set.

Something caused him to wake, and he opened his eyes. He thought he must still be dreaming. He thought he heard the same song he had heard so long ago in the forest.

Stumbling up on the sand, he moved nearer to the singing until at last he came to the miserable tumbledown cottage where Rapunzel was kept. She was singing in the doorway, looking with loneliness out at the darkening sea.

When she saw the poor, ragged man with blind eyes coming up from the shore, she recognised him at once and ran out to him, holding her arms wide.

"Rapunzel? Rapunzel?" whispered the prince, as she held him closely in an embrace.

Rapunzel began to weep tears of pity and joy as she cradled him in her arms, and the tears fell on to his eyes and healed them, so he was able to see again. After so much sorrow, the young couple were filled with great happiness to be together again.

The next morning the witch arrived at the cottage, travelling in a fine carriage led by two black horses. When she came into the cottage the prince and Rapunzel captured her and tied her up. Then they set off on the long journey home in the witch's carriage.

At last they came to the great palace gates, and the young couple were received with great joy by the king and the courtiers, who had given up all hope of ever seeing the prince alive again. The witch was banished from the kingdom, much to everyone's relief.

Rapunzel requested the king to find her parents, and after much searching, he succeeded. The old man and his wife were still living in the cottage overlooking the witch's garden, and they were overjoyed to be reunited with their daughter after so long.

The king decreed that the witch's huge mansion and wonderful garden were to belong to them, and they were guests of honour at the wedding. It was a marvellous occasion, a day full of feasting and joy.

Afterwards Rapunzel and the prince settled down happily at the palace until, when the old king died, the son became king of the land in his place. With Rapunzel by his side, he ruled well and kindly, and great happiness filled that country.

THE ELVES
and the
SHOEMAKER

Once, long ago in a pretty little village near a pretty little town, there lived a poor shoemaker, and his wife. They made their home in two neat little rooms above the shoemaker's shop.

No one in the village worked harder than the shoemaker, and no one was more honest than him. So you might have thought that he would be a rich man, with a thriving business. But, sadly, it was not so.

All the villagers were poor, you see, and much as they admired the shoemaker's fine boots and soft leather slippers, they just could not afford to buy more than one pair a year. The prospects looked bad for the shoemaker, and he and his wife lived frugally indeed.

At last came the day when the shoemaker had nothing left in the world except enough leather to make one more pair of shoes.

That night he cut out the leather by candlelight and left it on his workbench, ready to make up into shoes first thing the next morning.

Then he climbed up the ricketty wooden stairs to his two little rooms above, and sat down to the simple supper his wife had prepared. There was a basin of hot gruel, followed by some bread and their last piece of cheese.

Sitting by the fire together after their meal they talked about the sad state of their affairs. "I tell you this, my dear," said the shoemaker, with a small smile, "if things do not greatly improve tomorrow, I shall have to think about learning another trade."

"Come, let's to bed," said the shoemaker's wife. "It's a new day tomorrow, and who knows what it will bring."

As it turned out, no one could have guessed the strange and wonderful event which the next day brought.

The shoemaker went down early to his shop, and there on his workbench stood the shoes, already made! The good shoemaker was astonished.

He picked up the shoes, and he put them down again. He scratched his head, and he blinked his eyes. He went out of the door and came back in again. They were still there!

And, what's more, they were sewn as neatly as any pair of shoes the shoemaker had ever seen. The workmanship was truly of the finest quality. The shoemaker knew that he would have had to work hard and long to sew a pair of shoes as beautifully as these were sewn.

"Come here, wife! Quickly, come here!" he called upstairs, and his wife came running down, wondering what on earth could have happened to her husband.

When she saw the shoes she was quite lost for words. "Oh dearie, dearie me," was all she could say for a minute or two.

Then the shoemaker picked up the shoes and put them in the window of his shoemaker's shop, for all to see. And it wasn't long before the bell of the little shop tinkled brightly, and a fine gentleman walked inside.

"How much for those shoes, my man?" he asked the shoemaker. "I have never seen such a pair in my life."

Within minutes the shoes were sold, and at a handsome price. The bell of the shop tinkled once more, and the man was gone.

The shoemaker and his wife stood looking at the money in the shoemaker's hand.

"With this money, my dear, I can buy enough leather to make two more pairs of shoes," said the shoemaker. "I shall leave immediately, so as to reach the town before noon, and be back before sunset."

"Leave me one silver piece, husband, and I'll buy a fine bird to cook for our supper," said his wife. "We have something to celebrate tonight!"

It was a long journey to the town and back, and it was late before the shoemaker returned home with the leather.

He was tired from so much travelling, and he only worked for half an hour before going upstairs to enjoy the fine supper which his wife had prepared.

He left the leather on his workbench. It was all cut out, and ready for sewing in the morning.

At sunrise the shoemaker rose from his bed and went downstairs. And . . . can you guess?

That's right, the two pairs of shoes were lying on the workbench, beautifully sewn and ready to go on sale. The shoemaker didn't know what to think, but he immediately put the two pairs of shoes in his window, and within an hour or so both pairs were sold.

This time the shoemaker had enough money to buy the leather for four pairs of shoes, and that's just what he did.

That night, before he went to bed, he cut out the leather as he had done before, and left it lying on his workbench, ready to sew into shoes first thing the next day.

In the morning, the shoes were finished. This remarkable state of affairs continued for many weeks, and whatever the shoemaker cut out in the evening would always be finished by daybreak. The shoemaker's business prospered once more, and people came from miles around to buy their shoes at his shop, such was the exceptional craftsmanship with which they were made.

One evening, just before Christmas, the shoemaker told his wife that he would like to sit up and discover just who was doing this wonderful work for him. The shoemaker's wife agreed, and they hid themselves behind a curtain in the workroom, to watch and wait.

At midnight two little elves came in and sat themselves comfortably on the shoe-maker's tidy workbench. They were both quite naked. They didn't have any shirts, or any waistcoats, or any top-coats, or any trousers, or any shoes.

They picked up the pieces of leather which the shoemaker had left on the bench, and they set about their work, stitching and sewing and rapping and tapping at such a rate that the shoemaker could only watch in amazement.

On and on they worked, until the job was quite finished, and the shoes stood ready on the workbench.

And then the little elves simply bustled away, as quickly and as silently as they had come.

The next day, over breakfast, the shoemaker's wife turned to her husband and said: "Those little elves have saved our shop from ruin, and have made us rich. We ought to show them how grateful we are. I've had an idea how we can thank them."

"Do tell me, my dear," said the shoemaker.

"Well, I think it is sad to see them running around without a stitch of clothing on their backs. I am going to make them each a shirt, a waistcoat, a top coat, and a little pair of pantaloons. You can make them each a little pair of shoes."

"Why, I think that's a splendid idea," replied the shoemaker happily. "Let's start work straight away."

All that day the shoemaker's wife busied herself with her sewing, and the shoemaker busied himself with his shoe-making. The shoemaker's wife had never made clothes for elves before, and the shoemaker had never made shoes for elves either, but they both set to work with a will, hoping that everything would be just the right size.

There were many interruptions to their work, because by now the shoemaker's shop was the busiest shop in the village, but as soon as each customer had been attended to they went back to their work.

They had an early supper, and decided to give the elves their fine surprise that very night.

Just before midnight the shoemaker and his wife went down to the workroom, and instead of putting the usual pieces of leather on the workbench they set out their gifts for the elves.

Then they hid themselves behind the same curtain, to watch and wait once more.

Right on the stroke of twelve the elves came running in, flitting along on their tip-toes as always, and never making a sound. They scampered over to the workbench and were about to sit down to their work as usual.

The shoemaker and his wife clutched each other's hands tightly in their excitement, and tried not to make a sound as they peered round the curtain into the workroom.

In a trice the elves saw the gifts! And in a trice they slipped into the beautiful little shirts, and waistcoats, and top-coats, and pantaloons. Then they slipped their feet into the charming little pairs of shoes.

How happy and excited they were!

They danced and pranced and skipped and skidded around the room, congratulating themselves on how smart they looked, and doing little jigs and dances for the sheer joy of the wonderful surprise.

They were the happiest elves in the whole of the world that night, and the happiest shoe-maker in the world was watching them.

The elves never did do their sewing. For a full hour or more they whirled and twirled, and laughed and sang, and if you had seen them you would have said they were as bright and happy as sparkling moonbeams. It was a night to remember, that's for sure.

And then, as quick as a wink, and in the twinkling of an eye, the door quietly opened once more, and those dear little elves flitted through, out into the darkness of the night.

The shoemaker and his wife emerged from behind the curtain, and their eyes were glistening with tears. Tears of happiness, of course, because the wife's idea had been such a grand success.

The elves never came back again after that wonderful night. The shoemaker had to make all his own shoes again from then on, but he didn't mind that a bit. He had learnt a lot about shoemaking from watching those busy little fingers at work, and his customers never knew that different hands were sewing their fine shoes and boots.

He would have liked to have seen his little elf friends once more, but he knew in his heart that the ways of elves are not like our ways, and that he had been a very privileged man to have been visited by elves even once in his life. That is not granted to everyone, not by any means.

The shoemaker's wife missed the elves too, but she knew they would never come back. Why they had chosen to help her husband, the shoemaker, she would never know. But she did know that he had always been a good, and honest, and hard-working and kindly man, and she knew that such qualities are generally rewarded in one way or another.

She had enjoyed making those little clothes for the elves, and she began to take an interest in all manner of sewing, and soon became known throughout the land for her beautiful embroidery.

Many people asked her why her embroidery pictures often showed an elf, or two elves, or a whole party of elves, sitting on toadstools, or playing in the woods, or climbing up the stems of poppies and daffodils . . . Yes, many people asked her, but she never told the answer. That was her secret, and only her husband, the shoemaker, ever shared it.

Well, that just about brings us to the end of the story. The only thing left to tell you is that the shoemaker and his wife lived long and happy lives, in their neat little home above the shoemaker's shop. The business continued to prosper, and they never wanted for anything again. It was truly the happiest of happy endings.

Very often as they sat together in the evenings around their fire they would smile at each other as they recalled those magic nights when they had watched the dear little elves at work.

And how glad they were that the shoemaker's wife had thought of that fine idea to thank them. In all their years together, and however rich and prosperous they became, they would never forget their dear little friends, the shoemaker's elves.